St Thomas
of Yesteryear

Part One

Mavis Piller

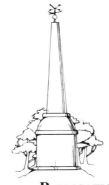

OBELISK PUBLICATIONS

OTHER TITLES IN THIS SERIES

St Thomas of Yesteryear, Part Two *Mavis Piller*
Ide of Yesteryear, *Mavis Piller*
Ashburton of Yesteryear, *John Germon and Pete Webb*
The Teign Valley of Yesteryear, Parts I and II, *Chips Barber*
Brixham of Yesteryear, Parts I, II and III, *Chips Barber*
Pinhoe of Yesteryear, Parts I and II, *Chips Barber*
Princetown of Yesteryear, Parts I and II, *Chips Barber*
Kingsteignton of Yesteryear, *Richard Harris*
Heavitree of Yesteryear, *Chips Barber*
Kenton and Starcross of Yesteryear, *Eric Vaughan*
Okehampton of Yesteryear, *Mike and Hilary Wreford*
Beesands and Hallsands of Yesteryear, *Cyril Courtney*
Exmouth of Yesteryear, *Kevin Palmer*
Sampford Peverell of Yesteryear, *Bridget Bernhardt & Jenny Holley*
Sidmouth of Yesteryear, *Chips Barber*
Lympstone of Yesteryear, Part One, *Anne Scott*
Lympstone of Yesteryear, Part Two, *Anne Scott*
Whipton of Yesteryear, *Chips Barber and Don Lashbrook*

OTHER TITLES ABOUT THIS AREA

The Lost City of Exeter – Revisited, *Chips Barber*
The Great Little Exeter Book, *Chips Barber*
An Alphington Album, *Pauline Aplin and Jeanne Gaskell*
The Ghosts of Exeter, *Sally and Chips Barber*
Exeter City – A File of Fascinating Football Facts, *Mike Blackstone*
Ian Jubb's Exeter Collection
Beautiful Exeter, *Chips Barber*
An Exeter Boyhood, *Frank Retter*
Exploring Exeter – The Heart of the City, *Jean Maun*
Exploring Exeter – The West Quarter, *Jean Maun*
Around the Churches of Exeter, *Walter Jacobson*
The Street-Names of Exeter, *Mary Ruth Raymond*
**We have over 170 Devon titles; for a full list please send an SAE to
Obelisk Publications, 2 Church Hill, Pinhoe, Exeter EX4 9ER**

Plate Acknowledgements
All pictures supplied by Mavis Piller apart from
Ian Jubb, page 18 (top),
and Dave Barrett, pages 16 and 17

*First published in 2001 by
Obelisk Publications, 2 Church Hill, Pinhoe, Exeter, Devon
Designed and Typeset by Sally Barber
Printed in Great Britain*

St Thomas
of Yesteryear

Part One

Having lived in St Thomas for many years, I have enjoyed collecting picture postcards of the area. It has also been a pleasure to collate them into the format you see before you – a pictorial journey through St Thomas of Yesteryear. It was such a difficult task to limit my selection of favourite views that this is just the first of two volumes!

The first picture is something of a 'red herring', as it is one of a number of postcards reproduced throughout the country, which had the same picture but with a different 'destination' depending on where it was sold!

The most obvious and natural boundary of St Thomas is the River Exe, so that's probably the best place to start our look at this densely populated parish as seen through the eye of the picture postcard photographer of yesteryear.

Below, only the lower part of the picture is St Thomas; the white, wide open space, centre left, is the former cattle market in Bonhay Road. It was located here until 1939 before moving to Marsh Barton. Nothing stays the same for long and the Marsh Barton site is now a retail shopping precinct, the cattle market having moved, yet again, to near the Matford 'Park and Ride' base. The card on which this view appeared was posted in 1935.

Courtney is still a common name in this part of Exeter. Here, on the junction of Cowick Street and Alphington Street, members of Courtney's staff stand at the shop's entrance. The large writing reveals E. M. Courtney's business, 'The St Thomas Drapery Stores' at 1 Cowick Street. The street directory for 1910 records Percy James Courtney as 'hardware dealer' at 3 Cowick Street.

Below is a wider view taken at the same spot, looking along Cowick Street towards the railway arch under St Thomas railway station. Note how much narrower this thoroughfare was in those days, there being no need for a dual carriageway along this once relatively quiet highway into Exeter.

The picture below clearly shows the tram lines, which begin quite a dramatic curve towards what was then a new Exe Bridge. It was opened in 1905 and was designed to be flatter than its hump-backed predecessor to allow the trams to pass over. The new single-span Exe Bridge was less likely to cause floods.

Above, an electric tram runs beneath the road tunnel under St Thomas station whilst a train is stopped above it. Car parking is advertised by a sign on the left, the fee being 6d per day (about $2\frac{1}{2}$p).

Below, a much wider, but rather featureless, Cowick Street can be spied, as buildings earmarked for 'new' shops and businesses are being constructed along the north side of this street in the early 1960s.

The problem of flat, low-lying areas beside rivers is that they are prone to flooding, as can be seen in these pictures taken in late October 1960. Above is a dramatic scene in a much-changed Cowick Street whilst below, it is almost impossible to recognise Alphington Street.

The flood waters caused immense problems in and around those parts of St Thomas closest to the river. The picture above was taken in Okehampton Place, which runs almost at a right angle to Okehampton Street. The car is a giveaway as to the depth of the water. It's interesting to note that a speculative fisherman trying his luck from the upper storey of his home, in this street, was lucky enough to hook a fish!

Here are two much older views of the river behaving itself as it flows beneath the towering cliffs of Bonhay Road. The Exe was a playground for many St Thomas folk and there were times, many years ago, that a swim in the river also served as a bath, many of the houses not possessing such amenties at that time. The swimming pool, shown below, was at Head Weir, very close to where the picture above was taken.

Although there are still corner shops in St Thomas many have been converted into houses. This picture postcard from about 1910 shows an excellent example, which stood on the corner junction between Albion Street and Okehampton Place. The shopkeepers were the Misses Maud and Lucy Diggines. Several decades later Mr Miller was the last owner to trade from this shop. Albion Street was originally called Victoria Street and then Albert Street. It's possible that the names changed to help the postal authority in its deliveries.

St Thomas of Yesteryear Part One

There is nothing on this card to identify the town or location, but Anne Scott, a postcard dealer who travels the country, thought it might be St Thomas. She called on me and said, 'I think it's your house.' Amazingly, when I checked the house deeds, she was proved correct! The name of Samuel Moore, who bought the house on 5 November 1900, is written on the window frame and he ran his bicycle business here in Albion Street.

I believe this to be the Seven Stars Hotel, shown above, which once stood near Exe Bridge but has long since gone.

Below, the King's Arms Hotel, as it was called then, stood alone in Cowick Street. It is still clearly recognisable, but the luxury of such a wide forecourt for parking disappeared, the cost of the road being widened in early 1960.

Here are two views of Exe Bridge when only one structure spanned the Exe to link St Thomas with the city. Some of the ornate lamps which stood on it were salvaged and can now be seen on Exeter Quay. The top picture was one of a series of informative cards, this being No. 9 of the Exeter Storyland Series, and bore these details: *The first bridge over the Exe at Exeter had thirteen arches, and was built on a weir by Walter Gervaise, a famous Mayor, in 1250. The second, which had three arches, and was completed in 1778, was replaced in 1905 by the single-span structure.* How this scene has changed! The message on the bottom card, posted to Oxford, said, 'We are now at Exeter and just going to the Hippodrome.'

These two pictures show the opposite sides of Cowick Street, looking towards the railway arch, but were taken in different years. Everything in the above scene, other than the bridge, has gone, including the Moreton Inn, the Turk's Head and even the car! Today the St Thomas Shopping Precinct, built in 1972, occupies the site.

Below, the suave Irving Taylor, of the former Swan Inn, issues this invitation to visit his establishment which, it would appear, was a 'Noted House for Home-Brewed Beer'. An electric tram, from Heavitree, is passing by. Beside this inn is Eastman's, the family butcher.

THE SWAN INN, ❧ ❧ ST. THOMAS', EXETER.
Noted House for Home-Brewed Beer.

Yours faithfully,
IRVING TAYLOR.

Meet me at
The Swan Inn
at................to-night.

The St Thomas Pleasure Grounds, off Cowick Street, were, in this genteel age, an ideal place in which to relax and unwind. Smartly-dressed individuals like these could spend time away from the hustle and bustle of street life.

Below, the tram has moved a little further along the street. This card, printed by Pollards, a well-known local printer, was posted on 3 May 1907 to a recipient who lived on London's busy Cromwell Road.

This aerial picture was taken during the early 1980s and even though it's a relatively modern picture, it still reflects a number of large changes which have occured since it was taken: towards the top right corner Haven Banks, once the site of visiting fairs, has witnessed the building of many new flats; a ten-pin bowling alley and shops have been built near the 'gasworks'; the former Willey's factory site has seen major redevelopment. On the middle right a large B & Q store has since appeared. And since the picture

was taken some buildings have come, had a very short 'lifespan' and gone again! Sainsbury's Exe Bridges Supermarket, just left of centre, is a classic example and the adjacent 'Plaza' has also undergone immense change, but mostly within the existing structure. The County Ground lies at the centre bottom; to its left, surrounded in trees, is St Thomas Church. The Methodist Church is in the extreme bottom left hand corner of this view, which was taken from about 1200 feet above St Thomas.

St Thomas of Yesteryear Part One

The electric trams ran along Alphington Road, providing a service to the city's outer limits. With precious few cars around public transport was, generally, well patronised as the trams trundled along a variety of routes. St Thomas, the flattest part of the city, was ideal for them.

Do you recognise this building? The caption has it as the Lion House Hotel, but if you are a regular traveller along Alphington Road you will know it as The Crawford, a country house until 1938, when it was acquired by the City Brewery. They converted it into a fine hotel. In 2000 it experienced major renovation work.

Below is a picture dated 9 January 1938 of the Exeter St Thomas Salvation Army Band. The bandmaster was Mr R. Northwood.

On this page we have two pictures, one of Class 5 and the other of Class 6, from 1910, taken at St Thomas Infants' School.

Here are two later pictures taken at 'Union Street School' with pupils sitting down to enjoy a Coronation tea in 1937 to celebrate the crowning, on 24 May, of George VI at Westminster Abbey.

St Thomas, with various venues, has hosted many sports. The next sequence shows just some of them. The picture of the St Thomas Amateur Rowing Club above shows the champion senior four of the West of England for 1907/08 showing off their silverware.

Below is Anderton & Rowland's 'Wall of Death', which was probably set up on Haven Banks, this picture having been taken about 1930.

Above, it's Empire Day 1910 and a time for much celebration. The advert to the right of centre is for Tighe's Ammonine, a medicine produced by the well-known local chemist and a revered remedy against colds and influenza.

Below, the 'speedway bikes' have no engines and there are more than four 'state-of-the-art' racing bikes lined up ready for the off! The County Ground has hosted many different events and sports including rugby, soccer, school sports days, and greyhound racing. Although the site had been previously used for various sporting activities the 'developed' stadium opened as the Devon County Athletic Ground Co Ltd in May 1894.

A huge crowd came to the County Ground to witness the Liberal presentation to Mr and Mrs Harold St Maur on Saturday 9 September 1911. It was the 'end product' of a rather unsavoury political post-election situation. In an extremely close-run ballot it was announced that Mr H. St Maur, relation of the Duke of Somerset, had narrowly defeated his opponent, Henry Duke (later Lord Merrivale). Duke was the son of a clerk who worked at the Merrivale Quarry, between Tavistock and Princetown, in the early 20th century. (There is a Merrivale Road in St Thomas.) When the result was given on 3 December St Maur's majority was slim in the extreme: 4,786 votes for St Maur, 4,782 for Duke. An election petition followed the recount, alleging that Liberal agents had voted, contrary to the law. It also stated the further objection that some 92 of St Maur's electoral supporters had been given employment for reward. The case was heard in January 1911 before Mr Justice Channell and Mr Justice Ridley. After hearing the evidence, they cancelled the vote of a local man who had boasted of voting twice and deducted four further votes for the illegal payment of election bills. The eventual outcome, in April, was that Mr Duke was declared the victor. The inscription on the presentation, which also included a tiara for Mrs St Maur, read as follows: *Presented to Richard Harold St Maur, Esq, JP, DL, CC by over five thousand sympathisers and friends in Exeter and the county of Devon in appreciation of his splendid services to the cause of Liberalism and to commemorate his victory at the poll, December 3rd 1910, and more especially to express their sympathy of regret that, as a result of some incomprehensible rulings in the scrutiny petition in April 1911, he lost his seat.* George Lambert MP made a speech and after the presentation a procession was made around the city.

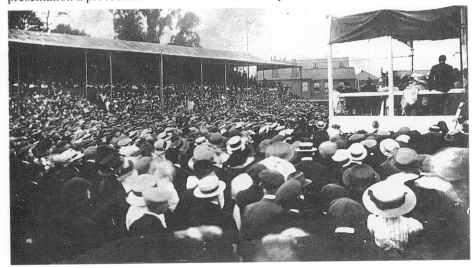

Exeter's 'Flying Falcons' have had many star speedway riders down the years but the greatest of them all was Ivan Mauger, top left, a New Zealander who won many world championships. Many rate him as the best speedway rider of all time. Here he is seen with one of his many trophies. He returned to the County Ground as a very special guest of honour at the Westernapolis meeting in September 2000. Top right is Colin Richards astride Jack Geran's bike in the 1953 season. Below, this pits scene from the early 1950s includes (from the left): Don Weekes, Tom Moxey, Ron Shears, Gerald Parr, Den Miller, Paul Moxey, Colin Richards, Johnny Fitzpatrick and Bill Dotton.

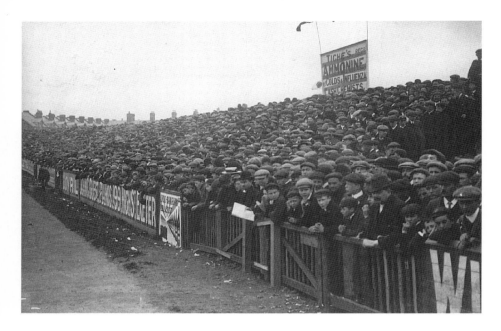

A vast crowd packed the terraces to watch Devon take on Durham at rugby union. Those who attended may well have arrived by the new electric trams, which had only been in the city a short time. One can be spied below, close to the Prince Albert (much later to be renamed The Roadhouse) and St Thomas Church. This would have been an appropriate point at which to alight for the County Ground.

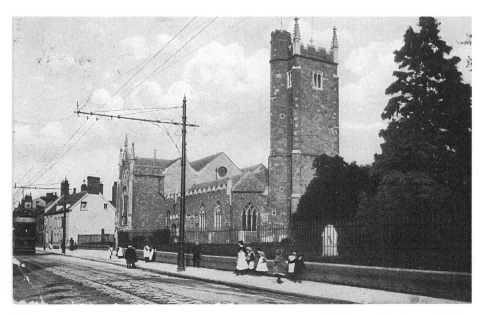

It's likely that the photographer took the picture because of the bus but it's the building behind it which will be of more interest to those who attended John Stocker when it was a secondary school. The building shown was the victim of a major blaze in November 1972. By the following June the bulldozers had moved in and cleared the site, now part of the John Stocker Middle School.

Below, older students will be more familiar with Crossmead, where there are now halls of residence and a conference centre for the University of Exeter. The house was built in the 1890s by James Langdon Thomas and the benevolent Plummer family lived here for many years. In 1944 it was bought by the University College of the South West.

Above, Buddle Lane looks a bit quieter than it is now. The same may be said of Newman Road, shown below. Opposite, the railway dominates these scenes, even the one taken in Buller Hall with youngsters dressed in Brunel-styled hats. This hall was named after Sir Redvers Buller, who commanded the British forces in South Africa during the Boer War. His ancestors, from 1739, were lords of the manor of Cowick. Many 'senior' locals will recall waiting for 'the Bathing Train', which offered a relatively cheap journey – sixpence – down to the sea for a refreshing and highly invigorating dip. At times this roofed station's platform was thronged with people looking to enjoy a day at the seaside. The railway line, when it was originally constructed through St Thomas, ran across the top of 62 arches, amounting to nearly a third of a mile.

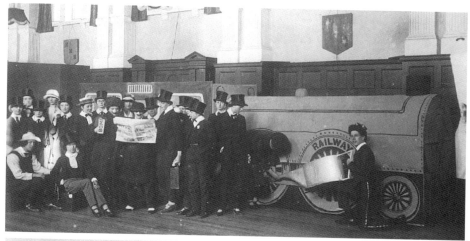

St Thomas enjoyed a building boom in the last decades of the 19th century. Between 1881 and 1891 the population rose by two thousand. This had its implications, particularly in a church-going society, where one packed congregation knew that their little iron church was inadequate. The new 600-seater Emmanuel Church rose heavenwards as the 19th century reached its end. The land had been kindly given by Sir Redvers Buller, patron of the living of St Thomas. A staggering 113 sets of plans were submitted, the 'winner' being that of Harold Brakspear. The design shown here was by Charles V. Johnson in 1896. The builder chosen was Mr Nicholas Pratt, based at Clyst St Mary. The bottom picture was captioned '"My Lady's House," Emmanuel Church Bazaar, 1909'.

(Opposite) If the King's Hall could talk, what a story would be told, because it has served so many different uses: cinema, casino, Quasar, place of worship, parachute factory, nightclub and so on. It was originally built as Emmanuel Church Hall. The *Flying Post* reported: *Next week it enters into formal possession of a remarkable*

building the like of which is to be found nowhere in the West; and no-one can say there are any compeers in the remainder of the country. The first fund-raising event was a bazaar entitled 'The White City'. The Mayor and Mayoress were in attendance to give it a boost, the target being £200.

KINGS HALL

Opened 2nd October 1912

SOUVENIR

The view from Redhills towards the city centre has changed considerably since this picture was taken in the days of 'steam'. In the foreground are allotments, with the railway just beyond them.

Below, it's a much colder scene – the River Exe having frozen in the bleak winter of February 1917.

If you have enjoyed Part One, there are many more fascinating pictures to see in *St Thomas of Yesteryear Part Two* …